"The creation of a thousand forests is in one acorn."
— Ralph Waldo Emerson

"Squirrels are the inadvertent heroes of forest restoration."
— Anne Raver

For my favorite Aunt Cathy – Beth
For Mom – Anna

Text copyright © 2019 by Beth Ferry · Illustrations copyright © 2019 by A. N. Kang · All rights reserved. Published by Orchard Books, an imprint of Scholastic Inc. · *Publishers since 1920.* ORCHARD BOOKS and design are registered trademarks of Watts Publishing Group, Ltd., used under license. SCHOLASTIC and associated logos are trademarks and/or registered trademarks of Scholastic Inc. · The publisher does not have any control over and does not assume any responsibility for author or third-party websites or their content. · No part of this publication may be reproduced, stored in a retrieval system, or transmitted in any form or by any means, electronic, mechanical, photocopying, recording, or otherwise, without written permission of the publisher. For information regarding permission, write to Scholastic Inc., Attention: Permissions Department, 557 Broadway, New York, NY 10012. This book is a work of fiction. Names, characters, places, and incidents are either the product of the author's imagination or are used fictitiously, and any resemblance to actual persons, living or dead, business establishments, events, or locales is entirely coincidental. Library of Congress Cataloging-in-Publication Data available · ISBN 978-1-338-18736-6 · 10 9 8 7 6 5 4 3 2 1   19 20 21 22 23 Printed in China   62 · First edition, February 2019 · The art for this book was created in colored pencil that was then scanned and digitally colored · Book design by Steve Ponzo

Squirrel's
Family Tree

by Beth Ferry
Illustrated by A. N. Kang

Orchard Books • New York
An Imprint of Scholastic Inc.

Squirrel gathers acorn seeds,
sturdy little oak nut seeds.
Anticipating future needs,
she gathers acorn seeds.

Squirrel hoards her acorns seeds,
scatter-hoards the nut-brown beads,
buries them in dirt and weeds,
those hearty acorn seeds.

Squirrel stores them in a cache.
(A cache is just an acorn stash.)
Watch the squirrel dart and dash
and fill each hidden cache.

Watch her also eat a lot.
She eats some acorns on the spot.
She nibbles with a plan and plot
to gobble quite a lot.

In a snap, white winter comes.
Snow falls down and cold wind numbs.
Squirrel eats up all the crumbs
as winter swiftly comes.

Squirrel does not hibernate.
She'll snuggle down and sleep in late,
but always she'll anticipate
the taste of something great.

And great describes those acorn seeds,
those yummy seeds her tummy needs.
Watch her hunt those hidden seeds
on which she plans to feed.

But many seeds she can't locate.
Her tummy will just have to wait.
And those seeds might just germinate
if found a bit too late.

Snowflakes melt and springtime sun
shines down warmth on everyone,
and something magic has begun
as winter's reign is done.

Squirrel sees a tiny sprout.
From acorn's shell, a sprout pops out.
Squirrel knows without a doubt
this sprout will soon branch out.

Soon the sprout is not so small.
A sapling grows up big and tall.
So many awesome things start small.
That's nature, after all.

Squirrel wants to make a nest,
a comfy, oak-leaf, twig-tight nest.
Moss and grass make it the best
and softest place to rest.

She settles in all cozily,
and quickly has a family,
and what a sight it is to see,
our squirrel's family tree.

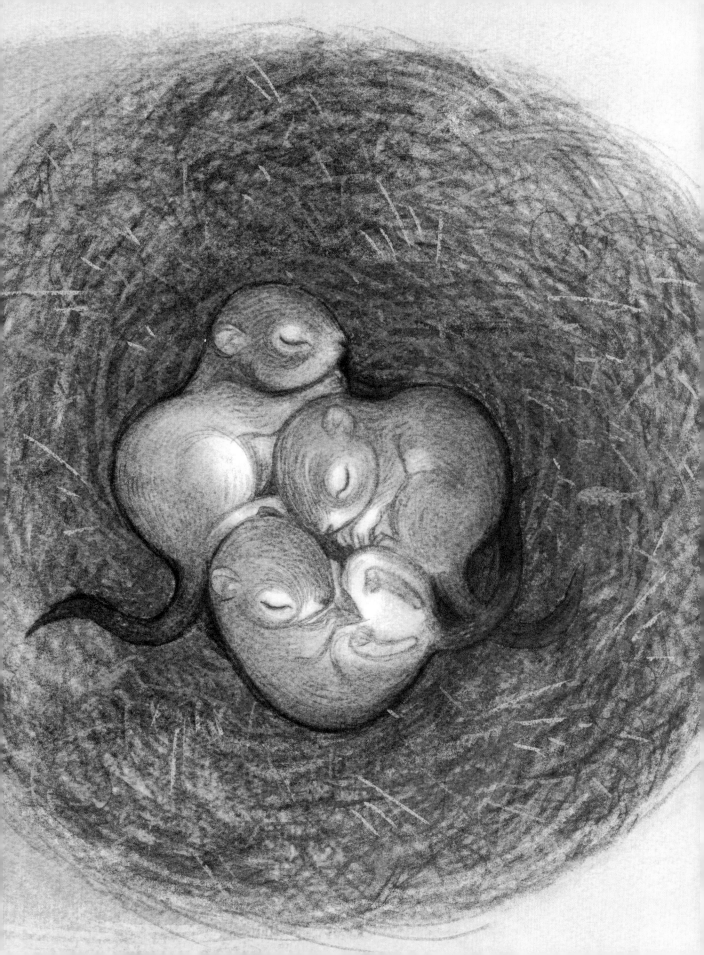

Squirrels come and squirrels go,
scatter-hoarding to and fro,
making sure that oak trees grow
and grow
and grow
and grow.

Without the oak, there are no seeds
that squirrels love and squirrels need.
There's much less chance they will succeed
without the acorn seed.

But squirrels also help the tree
by planting seeds haphazardly.
Squirrels are the heart and key
to oak trees yet to be.

The acorn cycle knows no end,
from seed to oak to seed again,
and trees and squirrels will be friends
until the very end.

Nutty Facts

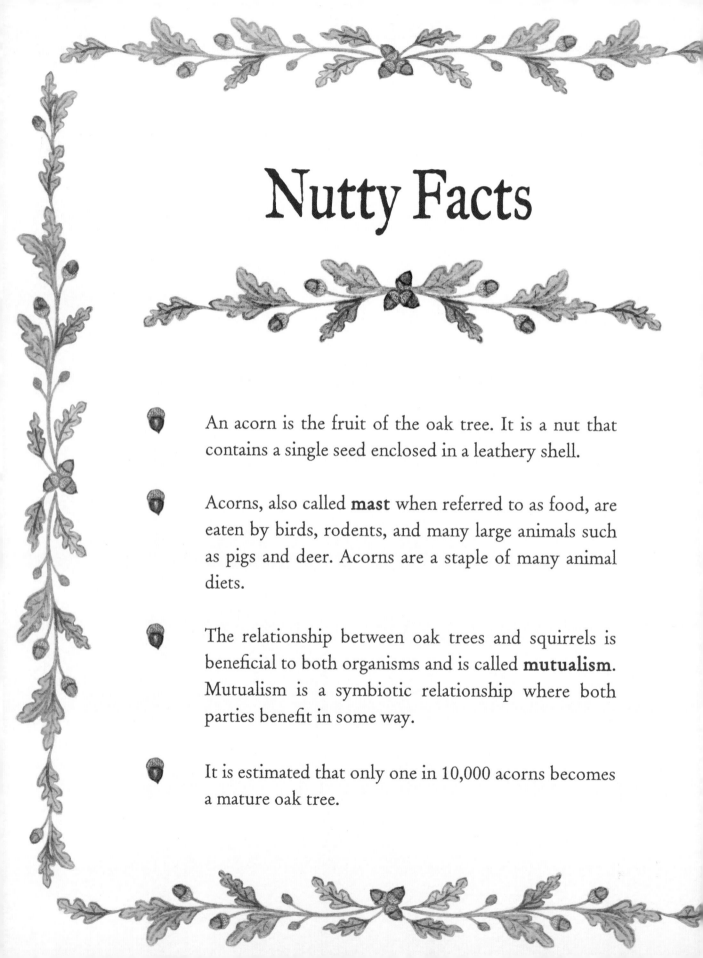

- An acorn is the fruit of the oak tree. It is a nut that contains a single seed enclosed in a leathery shell.

- Acorns, also called **mast** when referred to as food, are eaten by birds, rodents, and many large animals such as pigs and deer. Acorns are a staple of many animal diets.

- The relationship between oak trees and squirrels is beneficial to both organisms and is called **mutualism**. Mutualism is a symbiotic relationship where both parties benefit in some way.

- It is estimated that only one in 10,000 acorns becomes a mature oak tree.

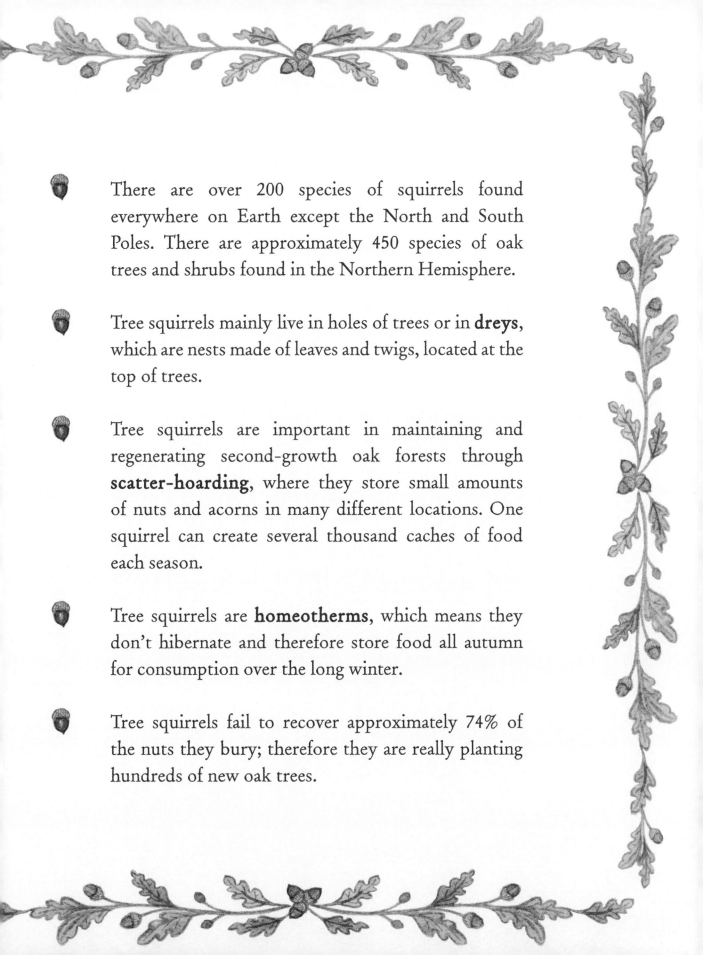

There are over 200 species of squirrels found everywhere on Earth except the North and South Poles. There are approximately 450 species of oak trees and shrubs found in the Northern Hemisphere.

Tree squirrels mainly live in holes of trees or in **dreys**, which are nests made of leaves and twigs, located at the top of trees.

Tree squirrels are important in maintaining and regenerating second-growth oak forests through **scatter-hoarding**, where they store small amounts of nuts and acorns in many different locations. One squirrel can create several thousand caches of food each season.

Tree squirrels are **homeotherms**, which means they don't hibernate and therefore store food all autumn for consumption over the long winter.

Tree squirrels fail to recover approximately 74% of the nuts they bury; therefore they are really planting hundreds of new oak trees.